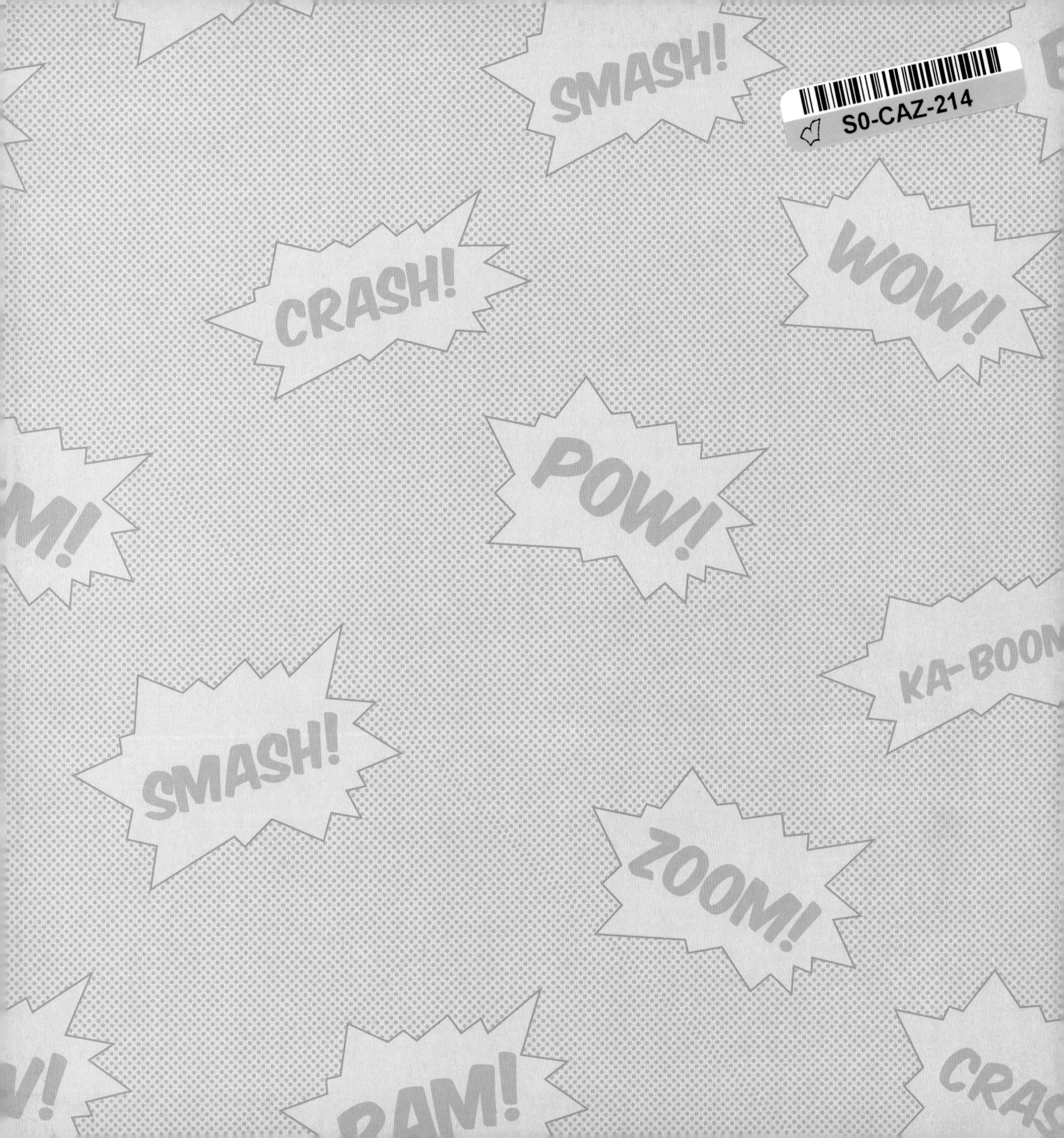
SMASH!
CRASH!
WOW!
POW!
SMASH!
ZOOM!

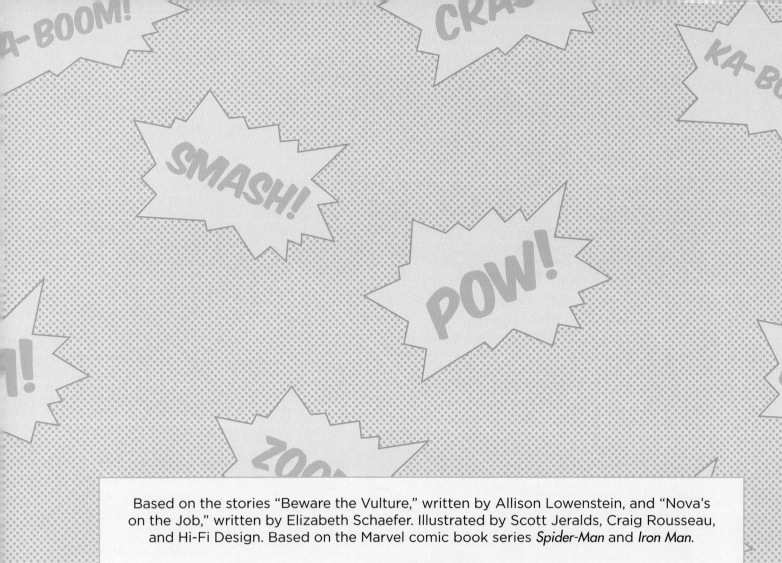

Based on the stories "Beware the Vulture," written by Allison Lowenstein, and "Nova's on the Job," written by Elizabeth Schaefer. Illustrated by Scott Jeralds, Craig Rousseau, and Hi-Fi Design. Based on the Marvel comic book series *Spider-Man* and *Iron Man*.

Printed in China
First Edition
1 3 5 7 9 10 8 6 4 2
978-1-4847-0290-1
T425-2382-5-13338

marvelkids.com

BEWARE THE VULTURE

MARVEL

New York • Los Angeles

Peter Parker and Gwen Stacy were eating sandwiches and enjoying the sunny day on the Great Lawn in Central Park.

"Isn't this so relaxing, Peter?" Gwen asked, and then pointed at the blue sky dotted with clouds. "You couldn't ask for a more perfect day."

Gwen was right. It *was* a perfect day. Then, suddenly, Peter's spider-sense began to tingle. Trouble was brewing somewhere in the city.

Peter looked up to see the Vulture soaring over Central Park.

Peter knocked over his water bottle in an attempt to distract Gwen. He needed an excuse to get away and change into Spider-Man.

"Gwen," Peter coughed, "I need more water." And off he went to save the day.

Meanwhile, at Stark Tower, billionaire inventor Tony Stark had just come back from testing his new Iron Man armor.

"How was the ride?" his assistant, Pepper Potts, asked.

But before Tony could answer, he saw the Vulture fly by his large glass window.

"Looks like we have a visitor," Tony said.

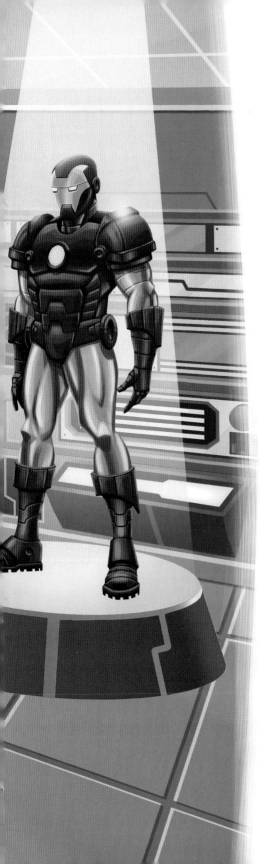

Suddenly, the alarm started to sound throughout Stark Tower.

"We need to protect the armor! If the Vulture gets his hands on it, he'll be as powerful as Iron Man!" Pepper shouted.

"I've got it under control," Tony assured her, and rushed off. But when he entered the lab, the Vulture was already there.

Without his armor, Tony was just a regular guy, and fighting the Vulture was next to impossible.

Just as the Vulture was about to attack, a voice called out from behind them.

"Back off, Vulture!" Spider-Man yelled as he swung toward the villain and delivered a mighty kick to his chest.

"Nice work, Spidey," Tony called out, racing toward his Iron Man armor. It was time to suit up!

The Vulture quickly got to his feet. He crashed through the window in an attempt to escape, but Spider-Man was too fast for him.

Spidey ran up the side of the building and fired a web right at the Vulture. It was a direct hit!

The Vulture flew away at top speed, lifting Spider-Man into the air.

Spider-Man needed help. The Vulture was getting away!

Far below them, police cars and helicopters arrived. They were responding to the alarms going off at Stark Tower. Spider-Man was glad to see them, but they weren't the kind of backup he'd need to take down the Vulture.

Suddenly a red-and-gold blur rocketed into the sky above Spider-Man. It was the invincible Iron Man!

"I've got it from here, Spidey," Iron Man said as he fired a repulsor blast at the Vulture.

"Thanks, I.M.," Spidey said, shooting a web at a nearby spire and swinging out of the way of the blast.

On the roof, Spider-Man and Iron Man teamed up to battle the criminal. Spidey shot webs as Iron Man blasted repulsor beams. The blows weakened the Vulture, who tried to fly away from the duo.

"Getting tired?" Spidey asked.

"Never," the Vulture replied.

"Time to clip your wings, Vulture," Spidey said, firing his webs at the villain. "You should know that crime doesn't pay!"

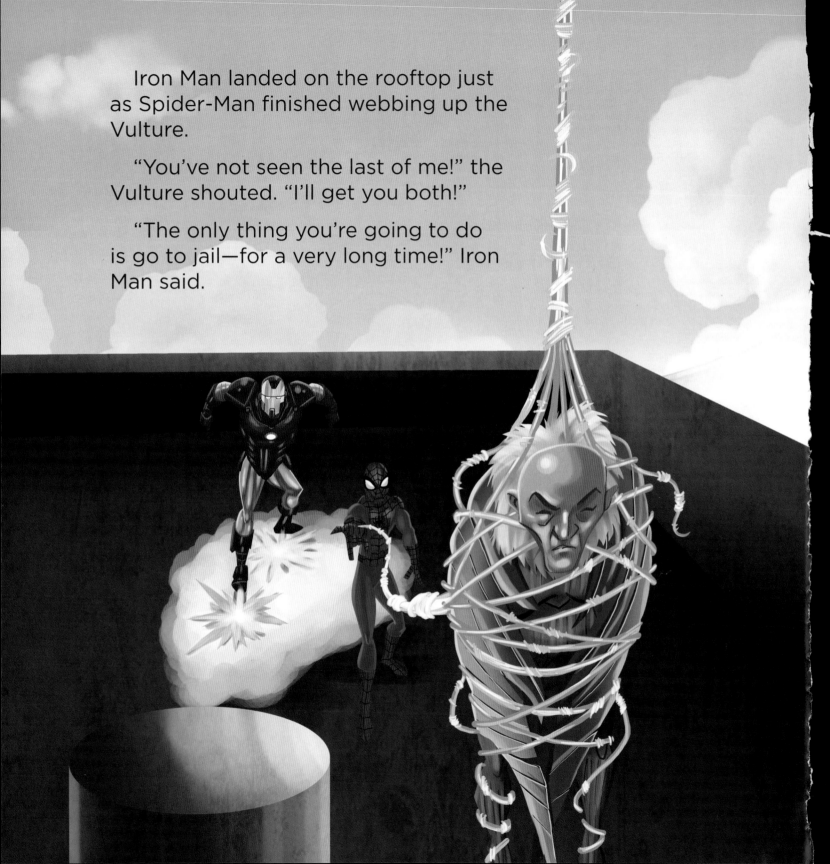

Iron Man landed on the rooftop just as Spider-Man finished webbing up the Vulture.

"You've not seen the last of me!" the Vulture shouted. "I'll get you both!"

"The only thing you're going to do is go to jail—for a very long time!" Iron Man said.

Later, after the police had taken the Vulture away, Iron Man said, "Thanks for the assist, Spidey. I've got to get back to Stark Tower to fix the security system."

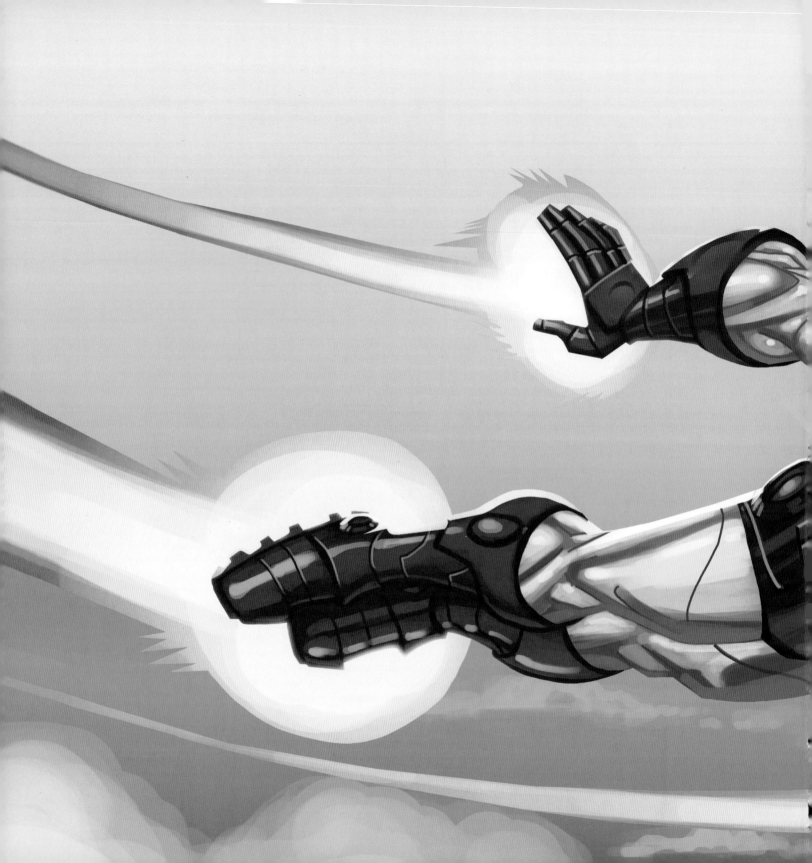

With the help of his repulsor technology, Iron Man blasted off across the sky at Mach speed. He had a lot of work to do if he was going to stop another villain from breaking into Stark Tower.

"I've got to get back to the park!" Spider-Man said to himself. "Gwen must be wondering what happened!"

Spider-Man swung over the city, glad to be done with the Vulture.

But Spider-Man's work wasn't done after all.

Below him, Spider-Man saw a little boy. The boy was all alone, and he looked very upset. Spider-Man swooped down to see what was wrong.

"I can't find Puddles anywhere—he's my dog," the boy said.

Spider-Man sighed. "At this point it will be tomorrow before I get back to Gwen," he said to himself. But Spider-Man knew he had to help the boy.

"All right, where did you last see him?" he asked.

Before long, Spider-Man found the boy's dog hiding in some bushes.

"Thanks, Spider-Man!" the boy said.

"It's what I do!" Spider-Man replied.

Finally, Peter returned to the park.

"You're back!" Gwen said. "What took you so long?"

"I had to help a boy find his lost puppy," Peter said, leaving out the part about helping Iron Man defeat the Vulture.

"Well, I'm glad you're back," Gwen said. "Today is one of those days where you just want to sit and relax with someone."

"I couldn't agree more," Peter said with a smile.

But Peter wouldn't be able to relax for long. Across town, the Vulture was making plans. "I'll break out of here," he swore from his jail cell. "And when I do, watch out, Spider-Man!"

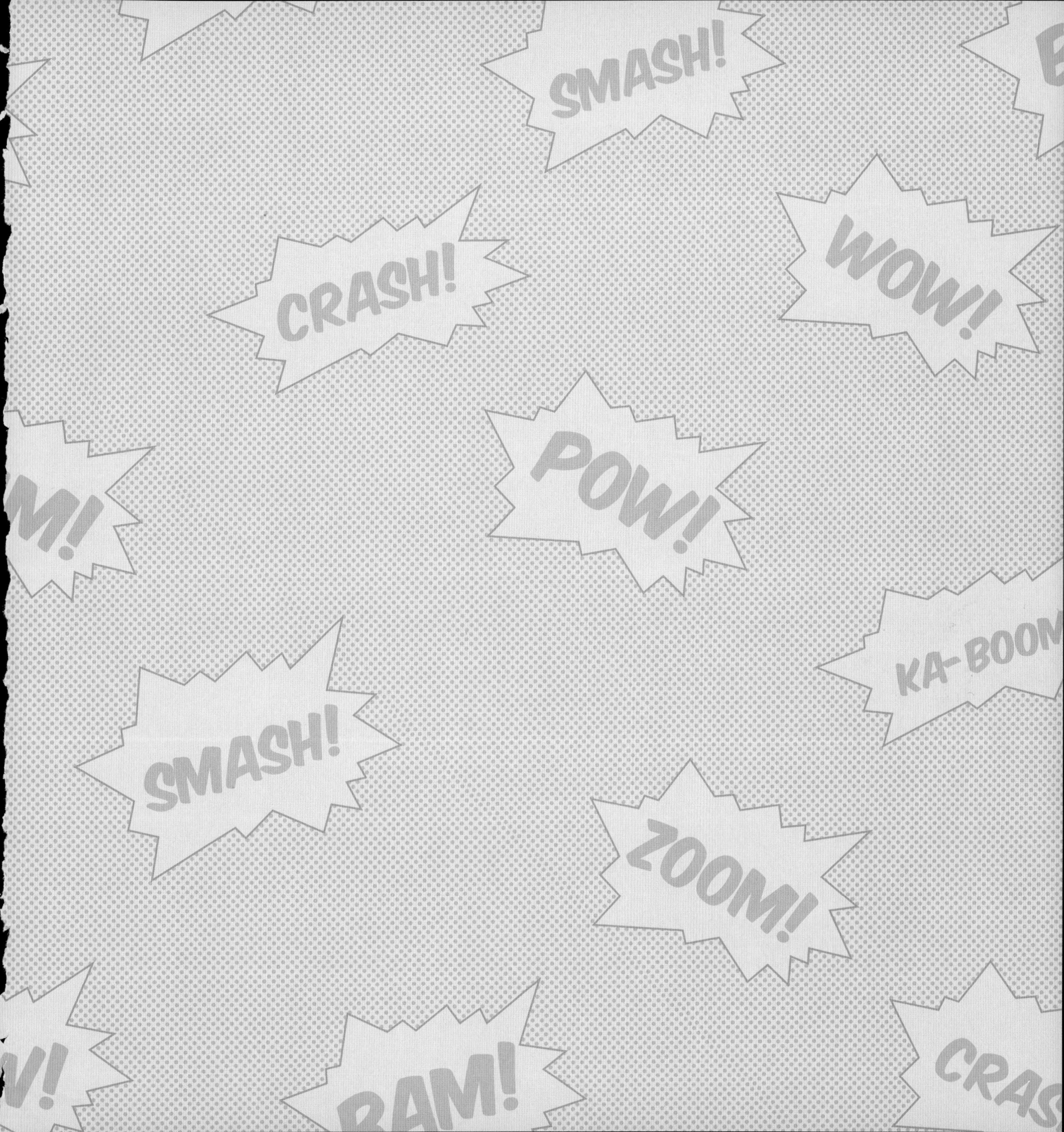
SMASH!
CRASH!
WOW!
POW!
KA-BOOM
SMASH!
ZOOM!

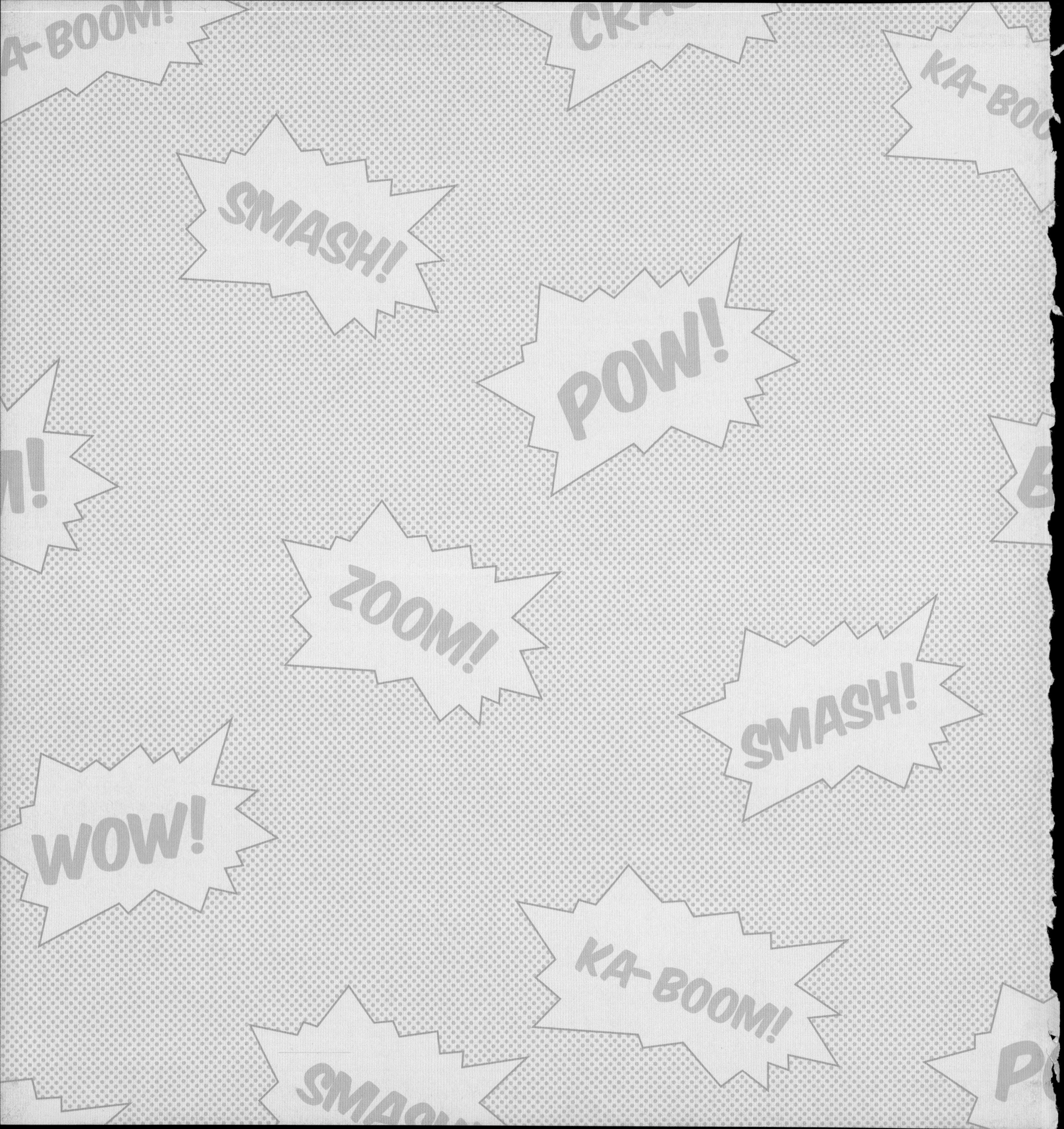
SMASH!
POW!
ZOOM!
SMASH!
WOW!
KA-BOOM!